Cover image by Youssef Naddam.
Find his work on Unsplash

Published by Naked Cat Publishing
https://nakedcatpublishing.myshopify.com/

Curl up with.
NAKED CAT
Lit. Mag
EST. 2023

Connections

Mathew Gostelow

For Zharain and Sofia

Contents

An Alignment

The sun's first light painted suburban clouds an unlikely neon pink. I jogged, energetic drum and bass bouncing in my earbuds. The tempo, a steady, unwavering one hundred and seventy-four beats per minute, suited my pace, feet pounding the pavement to the pulse of kicks and snares as I became one with the music, transcending the act of running.

I rounded a corner, beneath the electric dawn, and found myself snapped sharply from my trance, facing a squirrel. We both stopped, the squirrel and I, frozen, startled, each of us an alien invading the other's planet.

We stared at one another for less than a second. But in that second, I saw his perfect form, tensed, coiled, and ready to explode in rapid motion. I saw his large, dark eyes, and in them the sun's fluorescence reflected. Waves of light which left our closest star almost ten minutes prior - as I was tying my running shoes at the front door - and travelled a hundred million kilometres through the inky void of space, past planets, and moons, and more, arriving on the surface of Earth at just the perfect moment to shine in his black pupils and bounce to my own.

In that moment, I was aware that every element composing this squirrel, every building block in my own body, was forged in the furious fires of a distant sun, long-since collapsed. We were unified, joined by shared patterns of deoxyribonucleic acid, our elements singing the song of a supernova, much like the one that burned above us now, giving life to the planet around us. And I overflowed with wonder at this alignment, at the unlikely and chaotic series of ifs and buts and generations of births and happenings that led to both of us, the squirrel and I, being on this corner at this moment, staring into one other's eyes.

As this single second stretched to encompass aeons and lightyears, an ecstatic hip-hop voice in my headphones proclaimed: "Baddest mutha fucker on two turntables goes off!" An aggressive bassline and raucous clattering beat burst in my ears. The bass was a gnarled, distorted and filtered sawtooth wave, layered with a booming sub-bass, rich in frequencies that are felt rather than heard. I recognised the hectic drums as the Amen break, sliced to staccato hits and rearranged into an infectious rolling rhythm. I felt the weighty significance of this short drum solo - arguably the most important six seconds of audio ever recorded - sampled, chopped, sequenced and resampled again and again, taken out of context and baked into the DNA of drum and bass, jungle, hardcore, hip hop and beyond, all the way back to an obscure 1960s funk B-side. An instrumental by The Winstons, which became the cosmological genesis for post-modern music.

Adrenaline and dopamine shot into my blood stream, responding to the energy of the music, the familiar electro-chemical rush from the base of my spine to the hairs on my head. As I watched, the squirrel stood upright, staring straight through my eyes and into my soul, never breaking our connection. And I knew that he could hear it too, somehow. And he began to hop from foot to foot, in time with the ferocious tune, his front paws clenched to make tiny waving gun-finger gestures of dancefloor approval. I matched his movements, and the two of us performed a reggae-tempo half-step skank to the music. And as we moved in perfect synchronicity, I realised that we were one, and that concepts of 'self' or 'squirrel' were simply illusions. Too soon, the moment passed. The creature dropped and scrabbled into a nearby tree. I ran on, feet pounding in time, following my familiar orbit under a strange, vast, orange-pink sky, altered and connected to the universe in new ways.

Chez Nous

I approach the female maître d', wondering if that makes her a maîtresse d', but too afraid to ask. She is a snooty-looking woman, nose in the air, studiously ignoring me, wearing a 1930s flapper headband with a feather and six mismatched necklaces.

"Hello. I'd like a table for two, please."

She looks me up and down and then turns her attention to a small blue clipboard. Her nail polish is chipped. Bright yellow on one hand, green on the other.

"Sorry, we are full of books." Her voice is clipped, theatrically posh.

I'm disappointed. I've heard a lot about this restaurant and my wife and I are excited to try the menu.

"Oh no. I realise we should have booked in advance, but is there any chance you can fit us in?"

Another withering look. She peruses the clipboard again. I don't think it has any paper attached.

"We do have a table at ten past thirty."

"That would be amazing. Thank you so much. Should I... Errr. Should we wait here?"

She is annoyed now, impatient, barely able to conceal her

disdain.

"Come in and sit down here."

Of course. It's ten past thirty now. I feel so stupid.

She shows us to an uncomfortably small table and hands
me a menu, ignoring the fact that my wife is clearly not with
me. An exasperated look tells me we're expected to order
right away.

The menu looks like squiggles on blue paper. I struggle to
decipher its meaning.

"Can I have the... Umm... Chicken?"

"Yes." She appears to make a note on the clipboard. "And
would you like a cup of tea?"

"Yes please." I don't feel it would be acceptable to refuse.

The hostess earnestly takes an order from the empty chair
opposite me. My wife has also ordered chicken and tea.

The tea arrives first. We slurp it noisily as we wait for our
main courses, watching our server rummaging through a
box, where they apparently keep all the food in a big messy
jumble.

"It's nice here, isn't it?" I ask the empty seat, trying to make
polite conversation.

Our plates are plonked down roughly. Mine has a whole

roast chicken accompanied by a raw lemon, which rolls onto the floor before I can catch it. My wife's dish seems to consist of a small packet of cereal served with a floret of broccoli.

Under the watchful eye of our server, who hovers intimidatingly nearby while we eat, I feel compelled to enthuse over every mouthful.

"Mmmmm, so delicious!"

She takes our plates suddenly and without warning, before either of us has finished eating.

For dessert, we are served brightly coloured ice pops on sticks. There is no choice in this. The waitress keeps the strawberry lolly for herself and joins us at the table, slurping greedily.

Unexpectedly, she throws her clipboard to the floor. As I thought, it is empty.

"Your turn daddy," she exclaims. "You be the waitress now."

20/20 Vision

A foot pumps frantically on an unresponsive pedal.

"Sorry Billie, but that's nonsense. You don't have visions." Darren was in full flow now, his nasal voice a grating Styrofoam screech. "You have a vivid imagination and I'm sure you believe you're psychic. It must make you feel important, I suppose. But you have to stop kidding yourself."

A crunchy thud of impact, white noise crash, cries of alarm.

Darren's doughy face flushed blood-pressure red as he scoffed in patronising disapproval. Billie, carrying all the shopping, rolled her eyes but said nothing. It didn't take a psychic to know how that argument would end. Meanwhile, Darren's sausage hands were free to gesticulate as he walked ahead, lecturing.

An angry shark maw of jagged glass daggers glints in the sun.

"Come on Billie, I know you didn't go to university, but surely you're smarter than this. Look, I worked with an optician once who thought he could sense customers' thoughts during eye exams. Pure delusion of course. We let him go."

Pale desperate creatures rub their eyes in confusion.

Billie wished her visions of the future were perfect 20/20. Darren had appeared exciting at first, whisking her away from that suffocating small town. But his freewheeling confidence soon revealed itself to be just swaggering arrogance in a fancy, flowery shirt. And no matter what he said, when her random flashes of premonition did strike, they invariably came true.

A carnival cacophony of whistles, bells, and lights.

"It's your mother's fault of course. Filling your head with claptrap. Seventh daughter of a seventh daughter. It doesn't mean anything you know. Except that maybe Catholics need to rethink their attitude to contraception. Honestly, Guinness is the only good thing to come out of - "

Billie stepped back as the bus, brakes failing, mounted the pavement and slammed Darren through the plate glass of a bookie's window. The shocked punters inside winced at the sudden invasion of daylight and broken body. Billie shrugged.

It was a freak accident. Nobody could have seen it coming. The fruit machine in the corner began flashing, trilling and beeping. Someone had hit the jackpot.

How Time Travel Works

There's a telegraph pole on the corner that acts as a time machine. On hot days, the heady stink of creosote transports me back to the easy joy of that one sunny summer. Outdoor pool. Endless crinkle-fingered hours laughing, diving. My skinny pale self splashes with oblivious glee.

I'm desperate to show him the gathering clouds, reassure him that clear skies and smiles will return. But that's not how time travel works.

Automaton

In the knee-graze days of bikes and black ant tickles, my mum gave me a snuggle-buggle hug. That's when I heard a click-tick sound inside her, where her boomy-womby heart once thumped its beat.

The furniture at home was on the ceiling now. This change had made me cry and so she wrapped me in that clicking, ticking cuddle. She softly told me this was how our house would be, with furniture on the ceiling. I should get used to it, she said.

At that moment, a bombastic, brassy, one-man band boomed through the room, crash-stamping loud confusing sound. His face a squeaky red balloon with smile scrawled on in pen. He smelled of strangers.

Mum said the one-man band lived with us now. "Isn't his music nice?" she smiled, clicking and ticking in time. The honking, bashing din scared me, but I agreed because it seemed to make her happy.

I struggled to sleep that night, with my bed on the ceiling and the constant oom-pah, crash-bang racket he made. Mum was blissfully deaf to the frantic din. She didn't come to tuck me in.

As days went by my mother changed. Her hair was new red wire and smelled like sickly squirts of spray can oil. She moved in jerks with wringing hands. Her shiny face was frozen fibreglass apologetic smiles.

All the time, the one-man band was there, in every room at once, dotted lines of black ants creepy crawling in his wake. He loudly sang, aggressive, thumping drums to make me dance and skip. The big red happy smile balloon had smudged into a snarling ugly smear.

The house got smaller, daily, folding inward like a paper fortune teller. Room by stranger-smelling room it disappeared.

My mother shone translucent now, clockworks on display in flimsy shell. Her eyes were blinkered glassy beads, unseeing my exhaustion as I jigged along to please the one-man band.

Soon, her language jumbled unfamiliar, the tumble-tongue automaton. I struggled to make sense of booming strange words deep, like drainpipe echo man shouts.

The house was fortune teller folded to a single room. The furniture rained heavy from above, tables splinter crunching to the floor, scattering the ants that swarmed and crawled. The automaton was faded out to static fuzz, the blizzard of a detuned radio.

New wires and rods grew from the parping knees and crashing elbows of the one-man band. They moved the mother's hands and feet in time. His honking, barking voice went through a tube into her mouth. He blared and spat glass shards out through her cheeks.

That night I dreamed my mother waving at me from the shore. I swam and swam but currents dragged her deep and far until she disappeared.

I woke to find my home was gone. The ticking sound and oom-pah crash, no more. Just a folded fortune teller on the ground where it once stood. I picked it up to find my future out.

Moments

It's 9:05pm on 14th June 2008, and you're blowing my mind with temporal philosophy. We're drinking mint-muddled mojitos on a rooftop in San Diego and you're glowing with glee as you describe the elasticity of time. "An hour can pass in the blink of an eye, or a few minutes can contain a lifetime's experience," you say. "Gravitational attraction, if it's strong enough, can warp the fabric of space and time."

It's 7:27pm on 19th August 2007, and I'm salivating as you hand me a plate of aromatic, home-cooked tagine. We're at your flat in Cambridge, wind-borne dandelion seeds flurrying past the window. We just met, introduced by friends, but we laugh like we've known each other for years and I ask myself if you feel the connection too.

It's 9:08pm on 14th June 2008, and you're telling me the past, present and future are all equally real. "Every moment from all eternity is there, clustered together like the seeds on a vast dandelion clock." You grin, knowing you look a little unhinged as you gesture the shape in the air between us with your hands. "The present is just a spotlight moving across this four-dimensional sphere." My head spins, wondering if now, this moment in the spotlight, is the right time to say the words that burn inside me.

It's 7:37pm on 19th August 2007, and I'm dropping a forkful of tagine onto the carpet. I flush and cringe as I clean it up, but you smile and say: "Don't worry, a touch of ras el hanout is just what that rug needed." I laugh, but something sinks inside, knowing that I'll move to California next week, just moments after entering your dizzying, dazzling orbit.

It's 2:04pm on 9th June 2008, and you're emailing to say you'll be in San Diego for a conference. The months since I landed at LAX blew past in a blink. Our messages, tentative at first, gained gravity and acceleration as time flowed on. My heart takes flight on the breath of a second chance. This time, if I sense the same connection, I'll tell you how I feel.

It's 10:13am on 15th June 2008, and I'm driving back to Los Angeles, glowing from those slow-burning, joyful hours in the rooftop bar with you, sun setting and stars shining just for us. But a bitter black hole warps my mood and makes the journey drag. I failed to seize the day, scared the burning words would explode the fragile beauty of our moment.

It's 11:33pm on 13th August 2008, and you're eight hours ahead. We're talking on Skype for the third time this week and I just said: "I love you". You say it too. Our eyes lock through the screen. We're further apart, and closer together, than we've ever been before. The next second, swollen with emotion, seems to stretch eternal, but the call is over far too soon.

It's 11:36am on 26th April 2022, and we're in our garden, five thousand miles and fourteen years away from that rooftop. You say: "I fell for you the moment you blushed red, dropping tagine on the rug." Our daughter explodes a dandelion clock with her magical breath, sending seeds flying out through space and time.

Rewilding

At the morning meeting, colleagues stared aghast as shoots and tiny leaves burst through her skin.

By afternoon, the rewilding took hold – two huge fronds erupting from her back, unfurling winglike.

That night, she burst into a thousand floating seeds and allowed herself to drift away upon the moonlit breeze.

As the Halo Faded, So Did the Ghosts of Us

You missed it all – the halo of light in the midday sky, the echoes and projections. You were scouring the pebble beach for fossils when it happened. A timequake, they called it later.

Moments before, you stood triumphant, smiling with your cola-coloured eyes, showing me a flat round stone peppered with snail-like fossils, frozen for millions of years.

Your joy sparked my own and I marvelled at their beauty; white swirls and flecks against the ink-blue stone, like Van Gogh's night sky. Constellations and galaxies, dancing in the palm of your hand.

I thought of a phrase I'd heard years before, naming the stars 'šitir šame' – the writing of heaven. It was comforting to imagine our story printed clear and sure across the sky, fixed and waiting to be uncovered, like a fossil on a beach.

I flushed with affection as you crunched away deliberately across the stones, utterly rapt, back on your search. But even as I smiled, an icy nervousness fluttered through me. My hand, suddenly sweaty, reached into my jacket pocket, touching the box containing the ring. This was the same clammy panic I'd felt again and again, those last few months, bringing the ring to restaurants, the theatre, a walk in the woods. Each time, I'd convinced myself the moment wasn't right, the stars were not aligned.

It was a nearby star collapsing into itself that caused the timequake, they said – that halo flash like lightning in a clear blue sky. The gravity of it was enough to briefly shake the fabric of space and time.

Our pebble beach was filled with ghosts. You were looking down, absorbed, but I saw them. I cringed to see my past selves all around me. The podgy boy, too timid to stand up to playground bullies. The lanky teen; too desperate to be liked, too scared to talk. The quiet student hiding in his self-made shell.

Myself, standing, hand in pocket, touching the box with the ring two weeks ago, five weeks ago, eight weeks ago, frozen in the headlights of an uncertain moment, too petrified to take it out and say the words.

Our future selves were present too. I saw you saying yes – the two of us embracing on our beach beneath an exploding star. I saw you saying no. We turned with tears and walked our separate ways. I saw myself alone. I saw us playing with our daughter, her cola-coloured eyes sparkling with joy.

As the halo faded, so did the ghosts of us, until it was just you and I on that crunching pebble beach. I understood then. Our lives weren't fixed in stone, not written in the stars. We'd never know the future 'til we lived it.

I knelt among the pebbles, called you over, pretended I had found a stone full of fossilised galaxies. My hands trembled on the box as you hurried toward me, smiling.

The Helmet of Knowing

It was a metal colander, upside down, with yellow and green wires weaving through the holes. An elastic rainbow-coloured belt secured it to my head. Batteries poked from the sides, held in place with Blu Tack.

Paul Royce called it the Helmet of Knowing. He was a serious, pale boy with thick black hair, which his dad cut at home. He wasn't really my friend. Paul was a year younger than me and went to a different school. I only knew him from cubs, but for a couple of months, when I was eight or nine, we played at each other's houses a lot.

Paul's house smelled different from ours - fried eggs and aftershave. His room was too tidy. He had a deep bottom drawer full of bits and pieces, which he had raided to make the Helmet of Knowing. Solemnly, he applied the final components – two incredibly strong magnets from a broken set of speakers. He set one on each side of my head and they latched to the colander with a sharp clang.

"There. It should be working," he said, deadly serious. "How does it feel?"

In that moment, I knew it all. I answered in a robotic monotone.

"I feel all the world's knowledge rushing into my tiny human brain."

I knew advanced algebraic formulas. I knew the entire history of humanity. I knew the theory and practice of aeronautic engineering. I knew all languages, ancient and modern.

"Ask me a question," I said in my robot voice. "Ask me anything."

Paul's eyes lit up with excitement.

"What is three thousand, two hundred and seventy-six times four hundred and three?"

I pondered for less than a second.

"Thirty billion and forty-five point one thirty point five."

Paul giggled.

"And how do you say, 'Call me a taxi, my train is delayed', in German?"

Again, I answered almost immediately, this time in an overblown pseudo-German accent.

"Feertle der vangerschmus in das autoplopsch!"

Paul threw his head back with delighted laughter.

I wanted to show mum. I knew she'd like this. I loved to make her laugh - especially at that time, when dad was traveling, and her smiles sometimes seemed as far away as her stares.

I swaggered, grinning, down their narrow stairs, the Helmet of Knowing wide and wobbly on my head. When I burst into the room they were standing close, mum and Paul Royce's dad. They both looked at me, looked away, stepped apart.

In that moment, I knew it all. I felt the knowledge rushing into my tiny human brain.

I knew parents were just people. I knew they needed love, that they tried to do the right thing but sometimes got it wrong.

We didn't visit Paul's house after that. I never put on the Helmet of Knowing again. But once you've worn it, you can never go back.

Vertical Video

I wince at the alien sound of my own voice. We're bickering playfully in the clip. I'm awkward, pedantic. She's adorably careless, as ever. Her laughter is like birdsong. We're grinning care-free on a beach under cloudless sapphire skies – sea-tousled hair and skin sparkling with salt and sandy grains.

"You're doing it again. It's a crime against nature. Every time you record a vertical video, an angel dies – you know that, don't you?"

"Why? What's wrong with vertical video?"

She glints with gleeful mischief, knowing we've had this conversation a dozen times, knowing that a sliver of genuine annoyance hides beneath my jokes.

She wheels in selfie mode, turning the world around our fixed point in a joyful looping blur of cool seas, rugged cliffs, and golden sands. I stop the whirling with an arm around her waist. We are about to kiss, but the video ends abruptly before our lips meet.

Sitting alone in the strangely quiet house, I stare at this final image, frozen on the widescreen TV we chose together. The vivid picture of us lives in a thin strip, isolated between blocks of empty black.

Escape Velocity

I remember when they handed you to me. A blanket-bound bundle, eyes wide, alert, dark and bright all at once. A perfect baby girl. I was shocked at how something so small could evoke feelings so big - bigger than that stuffy room, bigger than the whole hospital, bigger than the sky, perhaps. So much love, more love than I thought possible. But also fear. I was terrified, in our first few minutes alone, that I would drop you, or hold you too tight and hurt you by mistake.

Picking you up or putting you down felt like an epic journey, an exercise in risky, calculated logistics. A few moments after you were born, you kicked one foot free of your blanket cocoon and I couldn't stop staring at your little toe. Curly and pink, like the tiniest shrimp you ever saw. I was so scared that I'd harm that toe before it even touched the ground. I imagined catching it on my clothes, saw it twisting round unnaturally. I broke out in cold sweats over something that had only happened in my head.

I get that same cold sweat now, as I think about what you're going to do.

I dreamed last night about the way we got you ready to walk to school on your own. Do you remember? We did it in stages. I started letting you take the lead, watching you decide where to turn and where to cross, making sure you looked both ways, checking that you knew the route. You were sure-footed, careful, confident. And day by day, I would leave you a little earlier on the journey. First I waved you off at the gates. Then across the road from the school. Then on the corner. Then by the post box at the end of our road. Until eventually I kissed you goodbye at the front door.

There was a lump in my throat that day as I watched you walk to the corner and disappear from view; part love, part pride, part fear. Those great big feelings they handed me, bundled in a blanket, they never went away. They grew bigger and stronger with each passing year.

When I woke, I realised that this gradual process, training you to walk to school, was always more for my own benefit than for yours. It was a way of letting go by degrees.

It takes an incredible force to leave the Earth's gravitational pull. The man from the agency explained it to me. They call it 'escape velocity'. On Earth, it's thirty-three times the speed of sound. That's three times faster than a bullet leaving a rifle, he said. I'm not sure why he thought that image would reassure me. Because the planet resists, you see. She wants to hold on to you, to keep you safely grounded, almost as much as she wants to see you fly free.

They're saying you'll be gone for nearly three years. Nine months that ship will carry you in her aluminium belly, before you land on the surface of Mars. You'll live there, on another world for almost a year, testing and experimenting and reporting back, before you begin your journey home.

Your feet will be the first to walk on Mars.

That familiar lump is back in my throat, all my feelings fighting for space inside it. They say the distance to Mars expands and contracts. Sometimes it's as little as thirty-four million miles. We'll get to talk then, when you're close. And even when our orbits pull us three hundred million miles apart, I know my love and fear and pride are big enough to bridge the void between us.

Mathew Gostelow (he/him) is a dad, husband, and writer, living in Birmingham, UK. Some days he wakes early and writes strange tales. If you catch him staring into space, he is either thinking about Twin Peaks or cooked breakfasts. He was nominated for the Pushcart Prize by *Spare Parts Lit* in 2022 and longlisted for the Welkin Prize in 2023. You can find him on Twitter: @MatGost

Milton Keynes UK
Ingram Content Group UK Ltd.
UKHW010851101023
430301UK00004B/90